All About Animals
Goats

By Justine Ciovacco

Reader's Digest Young Families

Contents

A Goat's Life on a Farm

A mother goat stores milk in her udder for her newborn. It can be tricky for a hungry newborn goat to figure out how to get the milk!

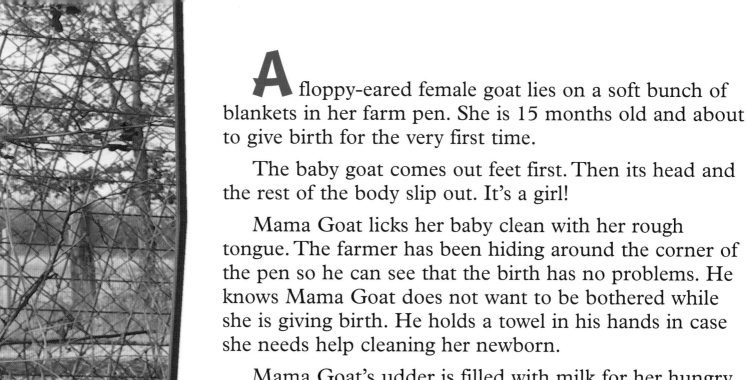

A floppy-eared female goat lies on a soft bunch of blankets in her farm pen. She is 15 months old and about to give birth for the very first time.

The baby goat comes out feet first. Then its head and the rest of the body slip out. It's a girl!

Mama Goat licks her baby clean with her rough tongue. The farmer has been hiding around the corner of the pen so he can see that the birth has no problems. He knows Mama Goat does not want to be bothered while she is giving birth. He holds a towel in his hands in case she needs help cleaning her newborn.

Mama Goat's udder is filled with milk for her hungry baby. The little one tucks her head under Mama's belly and sucks in her first drops of warm milk.

A week later, the farmer begins to feed the young goat cow's milk through a bottle. He needs to have Mama Goat's milk to make cheese and other dairy products.

Bottle Baby

On farms, baby goats drink cow's milk from baby bottles. A baby goat drinks milk until it is about three months old. Then it drinks only water.

The young goat is called a kid. Her favorite exercise is climbing on buckets and the fence that surrounds her home. She also enjoys chasing other kids in the farmer's meadow. Mama Goat looks up every so often to see her young one.

Mama and her kid spend hours wandering in the pasture, eating weeds and hay that are left for the goats in huge bundles. They always wander back to the cool, fresh water the farmer leaves out in big trays.

The kid is interested in learning about everything. She slowly walks over to any new item and sniffs it. Many times she will then nibble at it to see if it is familiar. She won't just eat anything. She will walk away if the item is dirty or tastes bad to her. And she does not like mint!

When she gets tired, she settles down in the dirt with another kid or Mama Goat for a rest.

Two at a Time

Dairy goats most often have two babies at once, but single births and triplets are common, too.

Friends
Female goats cuddle and spend time together.

Farm Family

Most goat farms are filled with female goats. A couple of males are kept separately. Young males are sold to other farms who want to breed more goats.

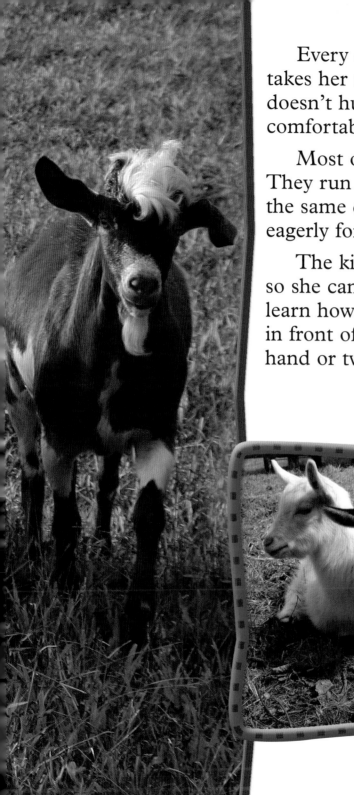

Every day the kid plays, eats, and sleeps. The farmer takes her aside every few months to trim her hooves. It doesn't hurt the kid. In fact, it helps her hooves grow in comfortably.

Most of the farm's one hundred goats stay together. They run in the same meadow each day and sleep in the same dirt pen at night. And each day they wait eagerly for visitors to feed and pet them.

The kid nudges her way up to the front of the fence so she can watch as the people walk by. She is eager to learn how they smell. She sniffs each hand as it passes in front of her face. Sometimes she takes a nibble of a hand or two just to see how they taste!

Help with Horns

A kid's tiny horns are often removed after it is a week old. They are burned off so the goats won't be able to use them to hurt one other.

Chapter 2
The Body of a Goat

Angora goats are almost completely covered with long, curly hair. Only their faces, ears, and legs below the knees have little hair!

Goat Hair

Goats are members of a group of animals called mammals. A mammal has a backbone, hair on its body, and drinks milk from its mother when it is born. Humans are mammals too.

Most baby goats are born with only a little hair. They need to stay close to their mothers for warmth until their hair grows in. Goats usually have white, gray, brown, or black hair, or a mix of these colors.

There are many kinds of goats, but they are all either domesticated (farm animals or pets) or wild. Dairy goats are raised for their milk. They usually have very short hair. Fiber goats, such as Angora and Cashmere goats, are raised for their soft, warm underhair, which is made into yarn for clothes and other products.

Most wild goats have short, light-brown or grayish backs and lighter hair on their bellies. The color of their hair helps them blend with the color of their surroundings, so they can hide from predators.

Going Gray
Goat hair sometimes turns gray as the goat gets older, just as human hair does.

Fabulous Footwork

All goats have good balance and are good climbers. Mountain goats are especially good climbers. They look carefully where to place their feet while they are climbing. This is very important in the mountains where there are high, steep cliffs.

Goats have special rubbery pads on the bottom of their feet that work a bit like the soles on your sneakers. The pads help stop a goat from sliding on smooth or slippery surfaces. Around each pad is a hoof, which is made of a harder material.

Mountain goats are able to make long, flying leaps from rock to rock. They land with both pairs of feet close together. These skills help protect them from wolves, bears, cougars, and other predators.

Making a Stand

Goats can stand on their back hooves for a short time without support. They also can stand upright while resting their front hooves on something in front of them.

Tree Climbers

It's quite a surprise to see a goat climbing a tree, but people have seen it! It's easiest for goats to climb if the tree is on a slight slope and not just reaching straight to the sky.

Mountain goats are sure-footed walkers. Baby goats are able to walk within hours of being born — even on steep, slippery, and dangerous cliffs like this one.

It's All Relative

Goats are closely related to sheep. One big difference is that most goats have shorter tails that stick up, but sheep tails hang down. Also, some goats have beards, but sheep never do. The horns of goats point up and back. Sheep horns curl downward.

Males and Females

Both male and female goats have horns that grow throughout their lives. The horns are not solid. They are empty, or hollow, inside. The horns of male goats are different from the female's horns. They are larger, heavily ridged, and curve up, back, and downward. Female horns are smaller, shorter, and usually point straight back.

Often only male goats have beards. One kind of goat, the ibex, has bearded males and females.

Only female goats have an udder, an organ that makes and stores milk. Baby goats drink milk directly from an udder.

The behavior of a goat is sometimes a clue to whether it is male or female. Although both males and females are social and spend time in groups, male goats prefer smaller groups and spend more time by themselves. Males are often seen on the edge of goat herds where they can watch for predators. Old bucks prefer to live alone.

Both male and female goats run from predators, but males are more likely to stop and try to scare enemies away.

Wild Words

A female goat is a **doe** *or* **nanny.** *A male goat is a* **buck** *or* **billy.** *Their baby is a* **kid.**

Eyes and Ears

The eyes of a goat are set far apart on its head. This positioning helps a goat see what is happening on either side of it, even when its head is lowered while eating grass and shrubs. Goats also have good night vision.

Most goats have ears that stick up and out to the sides. A few have unusual ears. Anglo-Nubian goats have long, floppy ears that hang down, sometimes to their jaws! The LaMancha goat seems to have no ears. But a closer look shows that it has tiny folds on top of its head that work just as well as the ears of any other kind of goat.

Smart and Sassy

Goats are very curious and smart. They can be trained to go to the bathroom only in certain areas, pull carts, and walk on leashes. Some people think that makes them great pets. But they can also get into a lot of trouble! Goats can sometimes figure out how to open farm gates, and they often nibble on anything that looks interesting.

The black pupils of goats'
eyes are in the shape of
small rectangles.

Chapter 3
What Goats Eat

Whether on a farm, like these cashmere goats, or in the wild, goats prefer to stay together as a group. A group of goats is called a trip.

Grazing in Groups

Goats usually stay together in herds or flocks. The herd is led by a female goat that people call the queen. Goat herds wander around hillsides and meadows, nibbling on grass, branches, and twigs. If they want to reach plants that are high above their heads, they can stand on their hind legs and stretch up for a short time without losing their balance.

Goats have tough lips and strong bottom teeth, so they have no trouble eating thorny plants. Their lips are flexible and slightly pointed at the tips. This is a big help because goats don't have any front teeth on their top jaw.

Goats that live on farms are fed a mixture of oats, barley, corn, and soybeans, as well as hay.

Mountaintop Munchers

Mountain goats spend summers in meadows that are high in the mountains where they graze on grass and bushes. In the winter, they travel down the mountain to be in a slightly warmer climate. There is less food in winter because of the frost, but goats will find moss and other plants to eat that are buried under the snow.

Special Stomachs

Sometimes goats move their mouths in an odd chewing motion, even when they are not eating. They look like they are chewing gum. What they are really chewing is cud. Cud is the food the goats have eaten earlier in the day and bring up to chew again to make it finer.

Goats do not chew their food thoroughly when they first eat it. They chew the food a little and swallow it. The food travels into the first two parts of the goat's four-part stomach. Later, the goat brings up the wad of food and chews it well. Then the goat swallows the food again. Now the food travels to the third and fourth parts of the goat's stomach to be digested.

Hoofed mammals with four-part stomachs that chew cud are called ruminants (pronounced *ROO muh nints*). Their special stomachs are able to digest rough plants.

Hair Balls

Goats swallow bits of hair when they lick themselves. The hair forms small, smooth balls in the goat's stomach. Some people believe the balls of hair can cure illnesses!

A goat's lips are important in grabbing food and bringing it into the goat's mouth.

Goats are such super
eaters that they can
completely clear an
area of anything green.
The bare ground can
stop a wildfire.

Goat Firefighters

Goats are such good plant-eaters that they are used to help prevent wildfires. In the western United States, hundreds of goats are sometimes trucked into dry, bushy areas. The goats munch their way across the large landscape of dry grass. They leave behind wide-open spaces of dirt, which can stop a wildfire in its path. A wildfire cannot move forward when there is nothing to burn. So the goats are able to help save people's homes and lives!

Goats are perfect for this job. They eat everything except the roots of the plants. Plant roots are important to the earth because they hold dry dirt together. Without roots, the dirt could blow away and plants would not grow. Goats will eat almost any plant matter in their path, including prickly cactus, sharp twigs, and poison oak that would kill other animals. In addition, goat manure droppings make the soil richer for new plantings.

All the President's Goats

President Abraham Lincoln received many gifts when he was elected president of the United States. His sons' favorite gifts were two goats named Nanny and Nanko. The boys, Tad and Willie, played with the goats inside and outside of the White House. The gardener was very upset when Nanny was found eating flowers in the garden!

Chapter 4
Products From Goats

An adult female goat stores milk in her udder. One female goat makes enough milk to fill a one-gallon pail each day.

Wild Words

An **udder** *is an organ that looks like a sack that hangs down from the goat's body. The goat's milk is made and stored in the udder.*

Goat's Milk

People around the world drink goat's milk and eat cheese and other products made from the milk. They also eat meat from goats.

A female dairy goat can give milk for at least ten months after giving birth. She then stops making milk for a few months until she is ready to have more kids and gives birth again.

An adult female is milked twice a day. Goat's milk is whiter and creamier than cow's milk. The milk can be used for drinking and cooking. It can also be used to make cheese, butter, candy, ice cream, yogurt, and even soap. One of the most popular goat cheeses is feta.

Goat's milk has more fat and protein than cow's milk. It is easier for people to digest than cow's milk. For this reason, doctors sometimes say that infants and people who get upset stomachs after drinking cow's milk should try drinking goat's milk instead.

The Big Cheese

The first step in making goat cheese is to send the fresh goat milk to the creamery. There it is heated to kill germs. At least a day later, clumps of thickened milk are separated from the liquid. The clumps are called curds. They are drained again and put into molds to be shaped into cheeses.

Hair's Your Sweater

The Angora goat's long white hair is called mohair. It hangs down in long curls. Mohair is silky but tough. It won't burn and, unlike wool, it is not eaten by moths. Mohair is very clear and can be easily colored with dye. People knit and weave mohair into sweaters, shawls, and other soft products.

The word *cashmere* comes from the province in India named Kashmir, where Europeans first saw cashmere goats in the 1800s. It is the fine, soft undercoat of the goats' hair that is used for cashmere products. Cashmere hairs can be combed off as well as sheared.

Both cashmere and mohair are warmer and less itchy than sheep's wool. They cost more than wool because one goat produces less cashmere or mohair than the wool produced by one sheep.

Hair or Hare?

If you have a sweater made of mohair, the mohair came from an Angora goat. If you have a sweater made of Angora wool, the wool came from an Angora rabbit!

The Finest Fibers

A special kind of cashmere called pashmina is found only on goats living high up in the Himalaya Mountains, which span Bhutan, India, Nepal, Pakistan, Afghanistan, and China. These fine, extra-soft goat hairs are dyed and made into shawls.

The hair from one Angora goat can weigh 11 pounds after it is sheared off. That's heavier than a human baby weighs at birth!

Chapter 5
Goats in the World

Goats can be found in very different places all around the world, from warm, sunny Hawaii to the cold mountains of Tibet and northern Mongolia.

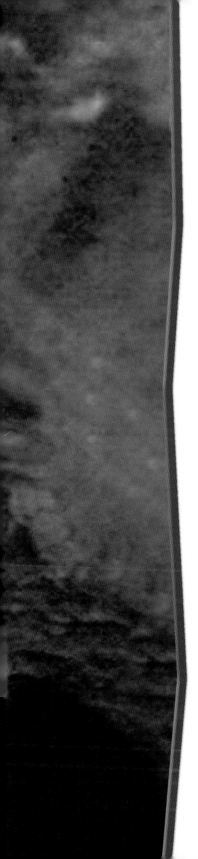

Where Goats Live

Goats and sheep were among the first animals humans took from the wild and tamed. That began around 10,000 years ago, most likely in northern Iran. Goats are mentioned in the Bible and pictured in ancient Egyptian art.

Today there are about 450 million goats in the world. Most live in Africa and Asia, but many others live in North America, Europe, Australia, and New Zealand. Because goats graze on grass and can survive in areas with only a little grass, they can live in almost every habitat on earth.

Fast Facts About Domestic Goats

Scientific name	*Capra hircus*
Class	Mammalia
Order	Artiodactyla
Size	Up to 40 inches tall
Weight	Females up to 220 pounds Males up to 275 pounds
Life span	8 to 12 years
Habitat	Grassy meadows and sloped hills
Top Speed	20 miles per hour

The Future of Goats

Goats may not be the strongest or fastest animals, but they are easy to care for as pets and to raise for a business. They give us food, milk, and material for clothes and other products. And they can help prevent wildfires.

Hunting by humans is not a big problem for goats in the wild. Many mountain goats live in places hunters have trouble reaching. Most goats are now born on farms. And although a few kinds of goats have become rare, there are still many goats in the world.

Going Forward

An organization called Heifer International gives families who live in rural areas around the world gifts of goats, cows, and geese. The animals give the families products to use and sell to make money. Families pass on the first female baby of each animal to another family in need.

For many goats,
life on a farm is
a cozy one.

Glossary of Wild Words

balance   ability to stand steady without falling

breed   to mate animals and raise the babies

creamery   a place where milk products, such as cheese and yogurt, are made

cud   food that comes back into an animal's mouth from its stomach to be chewed again

curds   clumps of thickened milk used to make cheeses

dairy   having to do with milk and milk products

domesticated   describing animals that have been bred over time to be tame farm animals and pets

dye   to change the color of something

flexible   easily movable

habitat	the natural environment where an animal or plant lives
hoof	a hard covering that protects and surrounds the feet of some mammals
mammal	an animal with a backbone and hair on its body that drinks milk from its mother when it is born
predators	animals that hunt and eat other animals to survive
species	a group of plants or animals that are the same in many ways
udder	the body part of a female goat that looks like a hanging bag where her milk is stored

Index